BEE·
TREE

BIG
STONES
AND
ROX

MY
HOUSE

EEYORES
GLOOMY
PLACE

OWLS
HOUSE

ND MR SHEPARD HELPD

Disney
Winnie the Pooh
Tales of Friendship Treasury

PaRRagon

Bath · New York · Singapore · Hong Kong · Cologne · Delhi
Melbourne · Amsterdam · Johannesburg · Shenzhen

First edition published by Parragon in 2012

Parragon
Chartist House
15-17 Trim Street
Bath BA1 1HA, UK
www.parragon.com

Written by Thea Feldman
Illustrated by the Disney Storybook Artists
Edited by Gemma Louise Lowe
Designed by Mandy Greenslade
Production by Emma Fulleylove

ISBN 978-1-4454-8944-5

Printed in China

Contents

A Bounciful Friendship

Tigger was having a *bounciful* day in the Hundred-Acre Wood.
He **bounced** this way.

He **bounced** that way.

He **bounced** this way again.

And then he decided to **bounce** over to Winnie the Pooh's house.

Pooh was cleaning out his cupboards and carrying his
honeypots outside. As he was placing an especially full
honeypot on the ground, Tigger bounced straight into
him. Pooh lost his grip on the honeypot, which crashed
into another one, which crashed into another one and
so on. The honeypots all tipped over and spilled.

"Oh, bother," said Pooh.

Tigger looked at the mess.

"That's quite a lot of sticky grass you've got there, Buddy Boy," he said, whistling at the sight of it all.

"Indeed," said Pooh, who began to try to get the honey back into the pots.

"Would you like some help?" asked Tigger. "Getting out of sticky situations is what tiggers do best!"

"No, but thank you all the same, Tigger," said Pooh.

"Well, seeing as you have your hands full, I'll go see what our pal Piglet is up to. T-T-F-N!" cried Tigger, bouncing off.

Piglet was searching the Wood for haycorns, which was one of his favourite pastimes. Piglet used the haycorns he found to make all sorts of delicious treats.

Suddenly, all the air was KNOCKED OUT of Piglet – and all the haycorns were knocked out of his basket. He watched as they rolled back into their hiding places.

Piglet felt a great weight upon him. That was Tigger.

"Hallooo, Pigalet!" shouted Tigger, bouncing off of Piglet. "What'cha up to?"

Piglet got up rather slowly, making sure that nothing in his little body had been broken by Tigger's big greeting.

"I was collecting haycorns," said Piglet, holding out
his empty basket.

Tigger looked in Piglet's basket. "Sure you were, little
buddy," he said, trying to be supportive. "Them *invisimible*
ones are my favourite kind!"

Piglet politely explained to Tigger that his basket had been nearly full until Tigger had **bounced** right on top of him. "Ooooooh," said Tigger. "Stopping can be tricky!"

"I see," said Piglet. He began to look for his missing haycorns – which was less fun the second time around.

"Well, it's a good thing this haycorn huntin' is somethin' you enjoy!" said Tigger. "I'll leave you to it!"

Tigger decided to **bounce on over** to Rabbit's next. As usual, Rabbit was busy in his garden.

Tigger didn't notice the rake right in front of him — until he **bounced** onto it and fell on top of Rabbit's plants!

Thud!

"You're **crushing** my turnips!"

Rabbit shouted.

CRUNCH!

"Why don't you go and **bounce** somewhere else?"

And so Tigger did — rather quickly.

While Tigger bounced somewhere else, he encountered
Owl, who was on his way home. Owl invited Tigger to join him
for a spot of tea, which Tigger happily accepted.

At Owl's house, Tigger took a sip that was more of a slurp.

"This is the *bestest* tea I ever had, Owl!" he cried. Tigger got up and bounced around Owl's table to show his appreciation, but somehow he also wound up showing Owl's teapot to the floor.

"Oh, dear!" cried Owl, who rushed to pick up the pieces. Tigger grabbed a napkin to mop up the tea, but ended up toppling the vase of flowers the napkin had been under.

"I think perhaps you had better leave now," said Owl, fearing for the safety of the rest of his house.

"Okay," said Tigger. "Leaving is what tiggers do best."

"Thank goodness for that," said Owl as Tigger turned to go.

Tigger went to find his little friend Roo, who liked to bounce almost as much as he did.

The two friends bounced happily in the yard until Roo had to go in to take a nap. Then Tigger waved goodbye and set off to find Eeyore.

"Hallooo, Eeyore!" cried Tigger, **bouncing** in so suddenly and loudly that Eeyore fell into the side of his house.

Crack! Crash! Twigs came tumbling down.

Tigger helped Eeyore up and brushed him off.

"I sure didn't expect *that* to happen," said Tigger.

"Neither did I," said Eeyore.

"Well, I could have predicted it," called Rabbit, walking up with Pooh, Piglet and the others behind him.

"Tigger, your bouncing is out of control!" Rabbit went on.

"But tiggers are bounciful when they're happy to see their friends!" Tigger explained.

Rabbit and everyone else knew that was true. But Rabbit was still annoyed. "You need to be a little *less* happy and a lot more respectful of others and their things!" he declared.

"That is, if you wouldn't mind," added Pooh. Piglet nodded.

Tigger looked around at all his friends. He looked at the ruins of Eeyore's house. The idea that his bouncing could make his friends unhappy was something that Tigger couldn't understand. Not sure what else he could say, he turned and walked away so that he could think.

Christopher Robin, who was on his way to visit everyone, came across Tigger sitting with his head in his hands.

"Whatever is the matter, Tigger?" said Christopher Robin. "You seem to have lost your bounce."

Tigger proceeded to tell the boy about all the things he had ruined in just one day. "I don't have an ounce of bounce left," Tigger said sadly. "I'm not sure I have any friends left either."

"Why, you don't really believe that, do you, Tigger?" asked Christopher Robin.

"I'm afraid so," said Tigger with a sigh.

"Let's go to find the others," said Christopher Robin kindly. "I'm sure you can mend whatever needs mending."

Suddenly Tigger bounced up!

"Christopher Robin, you are a genuine *gee-nee-us*! I'm going to mend *everything*!" he shouted.

"Hoo-hoo-hoo-hoo!" Tigger cried as he bounced off.

First, Tigger brought
Pooh new honeypots
brimming
with
honey.

Then, he filled an entire
basket of haycorns for Piglet.

Next, he planted some seeds in Rabbit's garden.

Then, he spent hours carefully gluing Owl's teapot back together.

He brought Kanga back her yarn, **rolled** into a nice ball.

And he rebuilt Eeyore's house all by himself. Most importantly, Tigger forced himself not to **bounce** – not even once.

"Well done, Tigger!" Christopher Robin said with pride.

"I must say I *am* feelin' pretty tiggerific!" said Tigger.

"Why aren't you bouncing then?" Christopher Robin asked.

"You *want* me to bounce?" asked Tigger.

"Wouldn't be you if you didn't," Eeyore said.

And so Tigger bounced – because it turns out that

bouncing *and* respecting their friends is what tiggers do best!

A Portrait of Friendship

Piglet painted pictures of everything in the Hundred-Acre Wood. He painted the tall, leafy trees, and the bright, yellow sun, and flowers of every size and colour.

One day, Piglet decided he wanted to paint what he loved most of all in the Wood: his friends!

Piglet asked Pooh, Rabbit, Tigger, Kanga, Roo, Owl, Eeyore and Christopher Robin if they would each sit for a portrait.

"Why, Piglet, I'd be honoured!" said Pooh. Everyone else felt the same way.

The next day, Piglet set up his studio outside in
the sunshine. He was ready to begin with Pooh.

Piglet soon saw Pooh heading his way.

"Hello, Piglet," Pooh called out, but he didn't stop.

"Pooh, wait!" cried Piglet, running after his friend.

"Where are you going? It's time to sit for your portrait."

Pooh stopped walking. "Oh, is that now?" he asked, a little bewildered. "I thought it was time to fill up my honeypot — and my tummy." Pooh gave his tummy a pat and looked at Piglet.

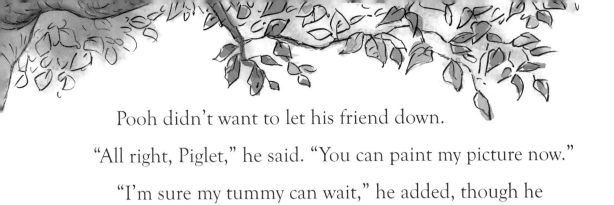

Pooh didn't want to let his friend down.

"All right, Piglet," he said. "You can paint my picture now."

"I'm sure my tummy can wait," he added, though he

was not at all certain.

"Now try to sit still, Pooh," Piglet said.

Pooh did. But his tummy did
not. It rumbled to the left and it
rumbled to the right.

Finally, Pooh's tummy rumbled him right up onto his feet.

RUMBLE RUMBLE

"Sorry, Piglet, but perhaps now is not a good time to sit still after all," said Pooh, as he picked up his honeypot and followed his tummy.

Piglet tried painting Rabbit next. He worked for a few minutes, then gave Rabbit a bunch of carrots to hold.

"These remind me of my garden," said Rabbit, jumping up. "And my garden reminds me that I have work to do. I'm sorry Piglet, but we'll have to finish another time." Rabbit hurried off.

Tigger had no trouble with Piglet painting his picture. The trouble was all Piglet's, since Tigger couldn't stop bouncing with excitement. "Sorry, Pigalet, but bouncing is what tiggers do best!" Tigger cried.

While Piglet waited for Tigger to stop bouncing, Kanga and Roo arrived. They were excited to have their family portrait painted by Piglet.

But Tigger was so excited to see Roo,
he snatched up his little buddy and the
two bounced off into the Wood.

Kanga proved to be good at sitting still for a little while. But before Piglet could finish, she suddenly gasped and jumped up. "Oh, dear! I must go and take my cupcakes out of the oven," she said.

Before leaving, she looked at what Piglet had done so far. "Why, that's lovely, dear. We will finish it soon, I promise."

Piglet was about to begin Owl's portrait when a note arrived for Piglet from Christopher Robin. It was good timing, since Piglet needed Owl to read the note to him.

"It appears that Christopher Robin's portrait will have to wait," Owl said after reading the note. "His young cousins are visiting with his family."

The mention of Christopher Robin's family reminded Owl of all the research he still had to do in order to finish his own family history. He flew off at once.

Piglet had much better luck with Eeyore, who sat as still and as grey as a rock.

"Eeyore, yours is the only portrait I've been able to finish," said Piglet.

"That's too bad," said Eeyore.

"Everyone else had too much to do," said Piglet.

"I'm just doing what I always do, too. Not much," said Eeyore.

Then, he lumbered off to do not much somewhere else.

Piglet thought for a moment.
"That's it!" he cried. "I need to paint
my friends doing what they *always* do!"

Piglet packed up his art supplies and
went to find Pooh. He painted Pooh
following a bee.

Then he painted several bees
following Pooh.

Piglet especially liked the painting he did of Pooh finally

getting a smackerel of honey.

Piglet went to Rabbit's garden next. Instead of asking Rabbit to stay still, he stood and painted while his subject moved about in his garden.

He painted several wonderful scenes of Rabbit at work.

Piglet painted Owl writing in his home library. Owl looked very deep in thought and rather intelligent.

As for Tigger, it gave Piglet a bit of a headache to follow his bouncing with his eyes. But he finally managed to paint Tigger's portrait.

At Kanga and Roo's house, Piglet started a new painting,
this one with the two of them together.

"Oh, dear," said Piglet. He sniffed his paintbrush.
"I believe I've dipped my paintbrush into the icing!"

It turned out to be a very cosy — and yummy — picture.

Piglet couldn't wait to show everyone his portraits. He invited his friends to view them.

Pooh and the others walked around and looked at one painting after another. They were very silent, which was unusual. Piglet began to worry.

Did his friends not like his artwork?

Finally, Pooh cleared his throat. "I'd like to say how wonderful your paintings are, Piglet." Then he looked thoughtful. "I'd also like to apologize."

"Whatever for, Pooh?" asked Piglet.

"For saying I'd sit still for you and then, well, not sitting still," said Pooh sheepishly.

Everyone else agreed with Pooh. Everyone except Eeyore.

"Thank you," Piglet said, "but sitting still isn't what *anybody* does best." He looked at Eeyore. "Except Eeyore, that is."

Piglet continued, "Everyone is good at something different. My paintings show you all doing the something you love best."

"And they will always remind me," he added, "of how lucky I am to have so many unique and wonderful friends!"

"That's right, Piglet," said Pooh. "So here's to each and every one of our one-of-a-kind friends!"

The
Sweetest
of
Friends

"Good morning, Piglet."

"Good morning, Pooh."

It was another day in the Hundred-Acre Wood. That meant it was another day for best friends Pooh and Piglet to be together.

"Pooh, I made some haycorn pie," said Piglet.

"Mmmm," said Pooh. "That will go lovely with some honey on top."

The two friends sat down and had a bite to eat.

When the last drop of sweet, sticky honey had disappeared
inside Pooh's tummy, he stood up.

"It feels like nap time," he said, as he usually did after having
a sizeable smackerel of honey.

Piglet answered, "I think a nap is a splendid idea, Pooh —
but perhaps you could be persuaded to take a walk first?"

Pooh stretched and yawned. "Lead the way, Piglet,"
said Pooh.

This morning was not unlike any other. Each day was a different adventure.

In the autumn, they played in piles of leaves.

In the winter, they made snow angels.

In the spring, they watched as the Hundred-Acre Wood became green again.

In the summer, they picked fragrant flowers.

Sometimes, Pooh and Piglet would visit their other friends together.

The two often went to Rabbit's house at mealtimes.

They listened to many a family story from Owl.

They helped Kanga with her knitting.

And they flew kites

with Christopher Robin.

Whenever Tigger invited Pooh out for a game of Pooh
Sticks, Pooh always brought Piglet along. This was just in
case Tigger followed Pooh Sticks with a game of 'bounce the
loser'.

Everyone in the Hundred-Acre Wood knew that
where there was Pooh, there was Piglet. And vice versa.

Rumble, rumble, rumble. Pooh's tummy always told him and Piglet when it was time for lunch.

"I believe I would like some honey, today," Pooh would say.

"That sounds like a splendid choice," Piglet would agree.

After lunch, they would spend the afternoon together.
Very often Piglet would watch birds and bees go by, while
Pooh snoozed against a nearby tree.

On this particular morning, Pooh and Piglet decided to pay Eeyore a visit.

"My, it's a lovely summer day," said Piglet.

"I suppose," said Eeyore, "if you like that sort of thing."

Rumble, rumble. Pooh's tummy joined the conversation.

"I do believe it's time for lunch," said Pooh.

"You're welcome to have some thistles with me," said Eeyore. "If you don't mind the crunch, that is."

Pooh and Piglet looked at each other. They didn't like thistles. But they *did* like Eeyore. So, they stayed and chewed on a few stalks with their friend.

When they left Eeyore's house, Pooh was still hungry.

"I believe I need something more," he said, patting his

tummy. "Perhaps just a pawful or two of honey."

Just then, a bee went by. Without hesitation, Pooh and his tummy followed it.

Piglet usually followed right after Pooh and his tummy. But, on this day, at the same exact time the bee flew in one direction, a beautiful butterfly fluttered by in another.

Without wasting a moment, Piglet ran after the butterfly to get a closer look.

And so, the best friends parted ways without even realizing it.

Through his binoculars, Piglet watched with delight as the colourful butterfly went from flower to flower. He looked closely at its lovely wings.

"Would you like to look at the butterfly with my
binoculars, Pooh?" Piglet asked, without looking
behind him. He thought Pooh was nearby, as usual.
"It's really quite a lovely creature!"

Instead of an approving snore, there was only silence. Piglet turned towards the tree where Pooh liked to nap. But there was no bear napping there. In fact, there was no bear there at all!

"Oh, d-dear!" said Piglet, alarmed. "What has happened to you, Pooh?"

Piglet wondered where Pooh had gone off to without
him. Or, rather, had Piglet been the one to go off without Pooh?
In either case, Piglet had to find his friend. He hurried
off. He wasn't sure where he was headed, but he knew
he'd be there when Pooh was there, too.

Meanwhile, Pooh had finished his encounter with the bee — or rather bees — and was having similar thoughts about Piglet.

Buzz

Buzz

Buzz

Not at all sure how he had wound up without Piglet *or*

honey, Pooh resolved to find first one, then the other.

Eventually, Pooh and Piglet came across each other on a path through the Hundred-Acre Wood.

"There you are, Pooh!" cried Piglet. "But, where *were* you?"

"I'm so excited to see you again, Piglet," Pooh said "I'm not quite sure where I was, only where I wasn't."

"Well, you weren't snoozing against a tree while I explored," said Piglet.

"That is precisely where I wasn't," said Pooh.

"I will make sure to say goodbye next time," said Piglet, smiling when he realized that there would be a next time.

"And I shall as well," Pooh said, equally happy.

"It would appear that together or apart, we're still the best of friends!" said Piglet.

"Yes, that is how it would appear," Pooh agreed.

"What would you like to do tomorrow?" asked Piglet.

"Perhaps we can meet for breakfast?" said Pooh.

"Oh, that's a splendid idea," said Piglet. "And then maybe we can take a walk."

"Wonderful!" said Pooh.

Under-the-Weather Friends

ACHOO!

It was a beautiful day outside in the Hundred-Acre Wood. But Winnie the Pooh was inside. Not only was he inside but he was in bed. What had started out as a case of the sniffles had blossomed into a full-blown cold.

Pooh's ears were a bit clogged, so he sneezed as loud as he could so that he could hear himself.

ACHOO!!

ACHOO!! ACHOO!!

Pooh's sneezes travelled through his open window and out into the Wood, where Piglet heard them. At first, it sounded like someone was calling, "Is that you? Is that you?" So Piglet responded, "Yes it's me! Who are you?"

Piglet followed the sounds until he realized that it was somebody sneezing. When he arrived at Pooh's front door, he realized that it wasn't just somebody sneezing. It was Pooh!

Piglet let himself into Pooh's house. If his best friend was sick, he had to help him to feel better.

Inside, he found Pooh making an odd assortment of faces.

"Pooh!" cried Piglet. "Whatever is wrong?"

It took Pooh a minute to notice Piglet.

"Well, hello, Piglet," said Pooh. "I'm afraid I can't hear you very well. I have a terrible cold, and it feels like there's more stuffing in between my ears than usual. I was trying to unstuff them."

"Perhaps a cup of hot tea might make you feel better," Piglet suggested.

Pooh strained to hear his friend. Piglet spoke louder.

"Why don't I make you a nice hot cup of tea? With HONEY?"

'Honey' was the one word Pooh managed to hear. And the steaming cup of tea did help a bit. Piglet spent the rest of the afternoon with Pooh, trying to take his friend's mind off his cold by chatting about this and talking about that. But Pooh still couldn't hear very much, and he dozed off and on.

The next day Pooh's ears had cleared, but his head still ached and he had to close his eyes repeatedly when he sneezed.

It was after one such series of sneezes that Pooh opened his eyes to find Piglet had returned, with their other friends in tow.

"Good morning, dear," said Kanga. "Piglet told us that you're under the weather. We've come to take care of you."

Pooh couldn't believe his good fortune to have so many kind and helpful friends.

Everyone got to work immediately. Kanga went into Pooh's kitchen to heat up a fresh batch of soup. Rabbit went with her to help her find just the right pot.

Clang! Bang! Looking for the right soup pot was very noisy when it was Rabbit doing the looking. Also, he and Kanga could not agree on which was the proper pot for warming soup, nor on the proper way to warm-up soup, nor on the proper soup to serve for a cold. Their loud voices carried their different points of view into Pooh's bedroom.

Now that Pooh could hear again, Rabbit and even gentle Kanga did seem rather loud. To make matters even noisier, Owl, who had positioned himself in a chair right next to Pooh's bed, was reading to him from a volume of Owl's family history.

ACHOO!!

Owl was straining to be heard over Piglet, who had resumed speaking to Pooh of the this and the that he had been telling him about the previous day.

Poor Pooh's headache was getting worse.   ACHOO!!

Then, Roo stationed himself at the foot of Pooh's bed, where he began to sing a special 'get well' song that he had made up all by himself. He had to start over a few times, because he didn't quite remember the right order of all the words.

Suddenly, Tigger bounced into the room. He was a bit late, but eager to help Pooh feel better.

"Hey, Pooh Boy!" cried Tigger. "I'm gonna do some bouncing just for you!" And with that, Tigger gave a stupendous bounce — and bumped into Eeyore, who was putting a bunch of flowers in a vase.

Clunk! Crash! Tigger bumped into Eeyore, Eeyore bumped into the table, and Pooh's vase and honeypots went crashing to the floor — along with Eeyore and Tigger.

"When a tigger is bouncing, it's a good idea to watch where you're standing," Tigger said as he tried to help up Eeyore.

"That could be why I'm sitting," said the donkey.

The sound of all his friends trying to make him feel better was making Pooh feel worse. His head felt as if someone was knocking on it.

The knocking turned out to be Christopher Robin, who had also come to help take care of his favourite bear.

Christopher Robin took a good look and a good listen. Then he clapped his hands to get everyone's attention. It took a few minutes, but at last everyone stopped what they were doing and gathered around the boy.

"I'm happy to see that Pooh has so many wonderful friends,"
Christopher Robin said. He glanced at Pooh. Pooh nodded his
head and smiled. And sneezed.

"But, perhaps," the boy said carefully, "you might each take a
turn doing something for Pooh — so as not to tire him out, that is."

ACHOO!!

Everyone thought that made sense.

First, Tigger and Christopher Robin righted Pooh's table.

Eeyore gathered up the flowers and put them in the vase. Piglet began to sweep up the mess.

Rabbit agreed to let Kanga serve her soup her own way.

"But," he insisted, "it will taste even better with a slice of carrot bread. I'm going to bake up a batch right now!"

While things began to bubble and bake in the kitchen, Owl sat with his book closed, and Roo softly sang his 'get well' song to Pooh from start to finish. Everyone applauded.

ACHOO!! "Thank you!" said Pooh.

Then Owl read aloud, while Pooh sipped soup and ate some fresh carrot bread with a smackerel of honey on top. Everyone listened politely to Owl's family history. Even Piglet, who continued to sweep Pooh's floors, made sure to pay attention.

ACHOO!! ACHOO!! Suddenly Piglet gave two extra-loud sneezes that startled everyone, including himself.

"It must be the dust from sweeping," he said.

The song, the food, the stories, the tidy house and, most of all, his friends, had made Pooh feel much better. By the end of the afternoon, his head didn't ache nearly as much and he was hardly sneezing at all.

Kanga plumped Pooh's pillows as the friends prepared to leave for the day.

ACHOO!! ACHOO!!

"We'll be back tomorrow to check on you, Pooh!" said Piglet, who was still a bit sneezy.

Pooh nodded, drowsy and content.

"It's lovely how you all fuss over me."

He sighed happily.

"It's what friends do, Pooh Boy!"

said Tigger as he **bounced** off.

"Of course it is," said Rabbit, who tugged on Pooh's

covers, smoothing them out before he left with the others.

The next day, Pooh was feeling much better. When his friends came to check on him, they found him dressed and outside, breathing in the fresh air.

"Why, it seems that your cold has gone away, Pooh!" said Owl, very pleased.

ACHHOOOOO
ACHHOOOO

"So it does," said Pooh.

ACHOO!! ACHOO!! The sound of sneezing came through the Hundred-Acre Wood. Everyone looked at each other, confused. Then they realized that Piglet was missing, and that the sneezing was coming from the direction of his house.

"Oh, dear," said Pooh. "It would appear that my cold has gone away, but not very far."

"Well," said Kanga, "now we know just what to do."

"We can all take turns making Piglet feel better!" Roo cried.

"'Cuz takin' turns is what friends do best!" Tigger said. "Hoo-hoo-hoo-hoo!"

Owl Be Seeing You

The Hundred-Acre Wood was abuzz with more than bees. Winnie the Pooh and his friends had each received a formal invitation to Owl's house. It read:

COME FOR TEA AND ANOUNCEMINT OF GREAT IMPORTENS.

"'An ounce mint'?" said Pooh, who enjoyed all sorts of sweet treats. "Why, that's very kind of Owl. Do you suppose that is a very large mint? And will there be one for each of us?"

Christopher Robin chuckled. "Silly old bear," he said. "I think this means that Owl has something to tell us. He's going to make an announcement."

"I see," said Pooh, but he wasn't quite sure that he did.

That afternoon, everyone gathered at Owl's house. Though he didn't see any mints, Pooh was content with the tea and biscuits Owl had provided, along with some honey.

"As you know," said Owl, "I have something important to tell you all. You may have heard me mention a reunion my family has been planning. It has taken a long time to plan due to the size of the family, the need to find a suitable location, a proper menu...."

Owl went on and on in his usual manner until finally Rabbit
stood up.

"Owl!" he said. "We know all about the reunion planning.
Every last little detail. But what did you want to tell us? Why are
we here?"

Owl stopped speaking for a moment. "Why, indeed?" he mumbled. "Oh, yes, I know," he said. "The reunion planning is all done. It begins tomorrow. I simply wanted to share the news with you — that I shall be gone for one week!"

"Don't worry about us. We'll be just fine while you're gone," Rabbit assured Owl as he and the others said their goodbyes. As soon as Owl shut his door, Rabbit clapped his hands together with glee.

"Don't you see?" exclaimed Rabbit. "We don't have to hear any more long-winded stories about Aunt Snowy or third Cousin Barney, twice removed! In fact, we don't have to hear anything from Owl at all for a whole week!"

While the others were less gleeful and rather more confused
about things than Rabbit, they were all somewhat relieved to not
have to listen to their friend go on and on — and on — about the
long-awaited reunion. It had proven to be rather annoying, as
had Owl's general way of lecturing about everything from teapots
to turnips.

While Owl was away, things went on as usual in the Hundred-Acre Wood. Rabbit tended his garden, only without Owl looking over his shoulder and talking nonstop about the glorious gardens his grandmother had when he was a young owlet.

Piglet painted his pictures, but didn't have Owl peering at each canvas and remarking on each painting.

Pooh still enjoyed plenty of honey, but didn't have to listen to Owl lecture him about the benefits of doing his stoutness exercises — something Owl had read about extensively.

It was also quiet over at Kanga and Roo's house. Kanga was able to bake in peace without Owl going on and on about what a wonderful cook his great-grandmother Gladys had been.

Roo and Tigger continued to play together often, but without having to stop for long periods to listen to Owl explain the science behind bouncing and other important concepts.

And Eeyore managed to rebuild his house – again – but without Owl boasting about the grand homes that some of his relatives lived in.

One day, after nearly a week had gone by, Rabbit was
in his garden. Over the past few days, he had begun to feel a little
lonely while working in it. Just then, two pesky crows swooped
in and began to peck at his plants. They had first arrived the day
Owl had left, and now they bothered Rabbit every morning.

"Shoo! Shoo!" Rabbit cried.

After he managed to wave the crows off, Rabbit thought for a moment. Perhaps, when Owl was around, it was too noisy for the crows.

"Well," Rabbit said out loud to himself. "Imagine that!"

As for Piglet, when he looked at the paintings he had done in the last week, he wasn't terribly pleased. He felt they were all missing something.

"Hmm," said Piglet, eyeing each canvas. "Perhaps Owl telling stories while I paint makes my paintbrush tell better stories."

Pooh was still rather enjoying his honey, but he couldn't help but wonder if it tasted a little less sweet without Owl around.

"I shall have to keep sampling smackerels to see if that's the case," he said. He was pleased to think that Owl would, no doubt, approve of this type of scientific study.

Kanga was finding her housework was taking longer and was much more work without Owl's company.

And now that Roo and Tigger could **bounce** to their hearts' content without Owl's lectures interrupting them...

...Roo realized that he got tired long before Tigger did.

"Don't worry, Little Buddy," said Tigger. "Bouncing is what tiggers do best." But the two friends found that they just weren't having as much fun as before.

Eeyore still managed to rebuild his house, but he definitely missed having Owl around.

"Seems like more work without the words," he said with a sigh.

Everyone began to wonder when exactly Owl would be coming home. The next morning, as Pooh licked the last of his breakfast honey off his paws, he realized that he wasn't quite sure if a week had gone by. Then, he realized that he wasn't sure how long a week actually was.

Pooh walked over to Owl's house to see if his friend had
perhaps returned already. He found Rabbit, Kanga and Roo there.
They had been wondering the same thing. Before long, Piglet,
Eeyore and Tigger joined the others. However, there was still no
sign of Owl.

"Does anyone know if Owl has been gone a week yet?"
asked Pooh.

"It certainly feels like a week to me," said Piglet.

"Why, it's more than that, I'm sure of it," declared Rabbit. He
thought for a minute. "What if Owl decides he'd rather live with
his relatives and never comes back?"

"That's *impossibabble!*" said Tigger.

"Isn't it?" Tigger looked around to see a bunch of uncertain, unhappy faces.

Suddenly the Hundred-Acre Wood was quieter than ever.
Everyone was thinking the same thing: Owl could be annoying at
times, but having no Owl at all was completely unimaginable.

Just then, Christopher Robin came down the path leading to
Owl's house. He was pulling his red wagon, which was piled high
with gifts. Walking beside Christopher Robin, talking up a storm,
was none other than Owl himself!

Everyone began to smile and, in some cases, bounce.

"Welcome back, Owl!" they all shouted as loud as they could.

Owl stopped talking. He was so touched by this greeting that he was something he had never *ever* been before – speechless.

When he could finally talk again, Owl said, "Well, it appears that you missed me after all!"

"We thought you might have enjoyed your reunion so much that you wouldn't come back," said Pooh.

Owl shook his head. "Oh, it was a splendid reunion," he said. "But, stay with my family? Never! They talk far too much!"

"Welcome home, Owl," said Rabbit happily. "Now, tell us all about your trip!"

Forget Me Knot

Winnie the Pooh hurried to the breakfast table. He did
this every morning, but today he was excited not only about
breakfast, but about the whole day ahead. He knew something
special was going to happen. That's why he had tied a ribbon
around his favourite honeypot — so he wouldn't forget. But now,
he couldn't remember what the something special was.

After a quick but satisfying breakfast, Pooh went outside.
He wanted to see the something special as soon as it arrived.
He took his favourite honeypot with him, just in case he
needed a smackerel or two of honey while he waited.

Before Pooh had been outside for very long, Piglet came whistling down the walk. Now, seeing Piglet was always something special. Somehow, Pooh was rather certain that today's something special was something else.

Just to be sure, Pooh said, "It's lovely to see you, Piglet. Pardon me for asking, but did we plan to spend today together?"

"No, we didn't, Pooh," answered Piglet. "But if you like, I can visit for a while."

"That would be splendid," said Pooh.

So, Pooh and Piglet spent the morning together. They whistled a few tunes.

And they played a spirited game during which they had to clap hands.

Then Pooh untied the ribbon from his honeypot so that he and Piglet could use it to play cat's cradle.

Pooh was having so much fun, he almost forgot that he was waiting for a different something special to happen.

"I don't remember when I've had such a good time, Piglet," said Pooh. "Except for the last time we were together. And then, there was the last time I saw Christopher Robin."

"Christopher Robin!" cried Pooh, sitting up. "That's the something special that's supposed to happen today! Christopher Robin is coming to visit me."

"What time is he coming?" asked Piglet.

"Umpteen o'clock, I believe," said Pooh, a bit uncertainly. "Is it umpteen o'clock yet, Piglet?"

"I'm pretty sure umpteen o'clock has come and gone, Pooh," said Piglet.

Pooh suddenly looked very sad. "There, there, Pooh," said Piglet.

"Christopher Robin was late once before," said Piglet. "Don't you remember? He was late because he was bringing you some honeypots as a surprise. He had so many that he had to pull them in his wagon, which slowed him down."

"That's just the kind of friend he is," Piglet added.

Pooh felt better in an instant. "I do remember that, Piglet," he said, giving his tummy a pat at the fond memory. "The boy is a rather thoughtful friend. And so are you!"

Piglet soon left, leaving Pooh to wait for Christopher Robin. Pooh couldn't help but wonder if his friend was late because he was bringing some sort of surprise.

Why, today could be about something special AND a wonderful surprise!

RUSTLE, RUSTLE! Pooh heard something coming through the Wood. Could it be Christopher Robin?

The something that emerged from the Wood was Owl. He had been out for a stroll in the fresh air.

"I've not seen the boy, but if he said he's coming, he is,"

said Owl. "You know how much he enjoys his visits with you."

"You are always the first one Christopher Robin thinks of whenever he has something new to share, such as a spinning top or a storybook," Owl reminded Pooh before he flew away.

Pooh smiled, remembering a story about bears and a little girl that Christopher Robin had once read to him.

After Owl left, Pooh kept his eyes on the path in front of his house. He was so eager to see Christopher Robin.

The next one to come by, however, was Rabbit, wheeling a cart loaded with turnips. "Would you like some, Pooh?" asked Rabbit. "I always grow more than I can eat. And when I think of someone able to eat more than I grow, I think of you."

"That's very kind of you, Rabbit," said Pooh, who then inquired about Christopher Robin.

"Well, he's probably just been delayed," said Rabbit. "If he weren't coming, he'd have sent you some sort of word. You know how he is. He's very loyal. I remember the time you thought that you'd lost your favourite honeypot." Rabbit gestured to the one on the ground. "That one, there."

"Don't you remember how Christopher Robin wouldn't go home until he helped you find it?" said Rabbit.

"Yes," said Pooh, remembering. "It turned out I had left it under a hive, hoping the bees would fill it back up with honey."

Rabbit went off with his vegetables, and a few minutes later Tigger came bouncing by.

"Whatcha doin', Pooh Bear?" asked Tigger.

Pooh explained that he was waiting for Christopher Robin.

"Oooooh," Tigger said, when Pooh had finished. "If it's Christopher Robin you want, it's Christopher Robin you'll get. Wait here, Pooh Boy. I'll go find him."

Tigger was gone for just a few minutes. When he came bouncing
back, he didn't have Christopher Robin with him. He had Eeyore.

"That Christopher Robin is nowhere to be found," said
Tigger. "But I'm sure this is just some minor *mixer-uperoo*. So,
I brought you Donkey Boy instead." And off Tigger bounced.

Eeyore sat down next to Pooh, and the two spent the rest of the day in companionable silence, until the sun set behind the trees.

Then, Eeyore got up to go. "Sorry he didn't make it," he said, as he started to leave.

Then Eeyore turned and looked back at Pooh. "Don't worry," he said. "That boy is a better friend to you than my tail is to me. You can't get rid of him so easily."

"Thank you, Eeyore," said Pooh. "You're quite right, I'm sure."

Pooh knew that Christopher Robin was a friend he could trust. That was why he found what had happened — or rather what hadn't happened — so odd. For the rest of the evening Pooh wondered and worried about Christopher Robin.

Pooh slept fitfully that night. He tossed and turned and dreamed that his pillow was a marshmallow. He woke up when he tried to eat it.

Pooh realized that it was morning. And that someone was gently pulling the pillow out of his mouth. It was Christopher Robin! The something special had finally arrived, and that was a wonderful surprise.

"Pooh," said Christopher Robin, "I know I'm early, but I just couldn't wait to spend the day with you today."

"Today?" asked Pooh. "Not umpteen o'clock yesterday?"

"Pooh," said Christopher Robin, "did you forget the date and the time again?"

"Do I do that?" said Pooh.

"All the time," said Christopher Robin.

"It would appear that I forgot that I forget," Pooh said.

Christopher Robin took the ribbon and knotted it around Pooh's favourite honeypot once again.

"Silly old bear," he said. "You're likely to mix up the details again. So, let this ribbon remind you that you can count on me, no matter what."

"*That* I shall never forget," said Pooh.

Seeds of Friendship

I t was spring time in the Hundred-Acre Wood. Everyone knew what that meant. The days got longer and warmer. The entire Wood began to turn green again. And Rabbit began to work in his vegetable garden.

Rabbit could think of nothing else. At tea with Owl, the plates reminded Rabbit of the cabbages he could be planting.

At Kanga's house, Rabbit thought of the flowers he wanted to grow.

When Rabbit was with Pooh, for some reason he couldn't quite

put his finger on, he had trouble thinking of anything other than

the squat, round pumpkins he grew every year.

Rabbit spent all his time in his garden. His friends soon noticed that they hadn't seen him for a while. He hadn't visited with Pooh or Piglet in days.

He had also failed to show up to bake carrot cupcakes with Kanga.

Rabbit was missing from Owl's
weekly geography lecture.

And Tigger couldn't recall the last time he had bounced
into his long-eared pal. Where was Rabbit? Everyone decided
that they should go check on him to make sure he was all right.

They found Rabbit on his knees, working away, digging and planting, even though he had nothing more than a lantern and the moon to shed light on his garden.

"Rabbit!" cried Owl. "What on earth are you doing gardening at this hour?"

"I can't talk now," said Rabbit. "There's so much to do and not enough hours in the day to do it all!"

"Rabbit," said Kanga, gently tapping Rabbit's arm, "you might be working too hard."

"Thank you for your concern," said Rabbit. "But there's no way around it. I simply must plant my turnips and radishes and then start on my carrots and cucumbers."

"Perhaps you could use some assistance," suggested Owl.

"Of course that's what I need," said Rabbit. "But where will I find good, reliable workers who will do as I say?"

"Helloooo?!" said Tigger, waving his arms and bouncing. "You must be awfully tired, Long Ears. There's a whole bunch of *helperators* right here."

Rabbit looked around but didn't see anyone except his friends. "Helpers?" Rabbit said, puzzled.

"Team Rabbit at your service!" said Tigger. The others smiled and nodded.

Rabbit looked at all the eager, friendly faces. Then he sighed and said, "I do need some sleep. All right, report for duty in the morning."

Bright and early the next morning, everyone arrived at Rabbit's house, ready to work. Rabbit, refreshed after a good night's sleep, rubbed his hands together while figuring out how to best use everyone's strengths in the tasks ahead.

In no time at all, he had Piglet raking a patch of ground,
clearing away rocks and smoothing the soil.

"This is a lot like sweeping," Piglet said. "And I do enjoy that."

Next, Rabbit had Roo dig holes for seeds. Owl watched

from a tree to make sure Roo dug the holes in neat little rows.

"Splendid work, Roo!" said Rabbit.

"Thank you, Rabbit," said Roo, while Kanga beamed. To Roo,

it didn't feel like work at all. It felt like he was playing

in a giant sandbox!

Kanga followed Roo and carefully placed the proper seeds into each freshly dug hole.

Then Pooh followed behind Kanga and filled each hole with dirt.

"That's it, Pooh," said Rabbit. "Think of it just like filling your
tummy with honey."

"What a lovely thought, Rabbit," said Pooh, who started to pile
the soil in quicker and higher.

"Hoo-hoo-hoo-hoo!" shouted Tigger. "Here comes *gardenatin'* at its best!"

Thump Thump Thump

With that, Tigger started bouncing on the little soil mounds to make sure they were packed down tightly around the seeds.

Rabbit smiled. "At last," he said under his breath, "a constructive use of Tigger's, er, talents."

Rabbit could not believe how quickly his entire garden was planted. He had to admit, having a team of friends to help him made the task easier — and more entertaining — than ever before.

When the planting was done, Rabbit hosted a thank you party for his friends. In no time, the team was able to see the results of their hard work. Little stems and buds began to grow.

But Rabbit and his friends were not the only ones to notice. Big, buzzing honeybees began visiting the garden. A lot of them.

Now, just like every good gardener, Rabbit knew that bees were good for his plants and flowers. But there were just so many of them... buzzing, buzzing, buzzing everywhere.

"Shoo, shoo!" he cried, waving at the noisy honeybees. But Rabbit couldn't get even one bee to leave.

Just then, Pooh came by to check on the garden's progress.

"Ah, Pooh," Rabbit said. "You should know a thing or two about bees. Can you do something to get rid of them?"

Pooh thought for a moment. Then he said, "Perhaps if I run, they will chase after me. That seems to be something bees enjoy doing." So, Pooh turned and ran away from Rabbit's garden as fast as he could. But the bees didn't pay any attention to him.

Pooh didn't stop running until he came across Christopher
Robin walking through the Wood. Once Pooh caught his breath,
he explained the problem of the unwanted visitors in Rabbit's
garden. Then he explained why he was running.

"Silly old bear," said Christopher Robin. "Bees only chase you when you're bothering their hive."

"Oh, bother," said Pooh.

"Besides," said the boy as they walked to Rabbit's garden together, "it sounds like the bees are just doing their jobs. You know they help gardens grow, right Pooh?"

"I do," said Pooh, even though his own experience with bees was usually limited to getting honey and trying not to get stung.

"Pooh, I've still got every single bee I had before you ran out of here," said Rabbit when Pooh arrived with Christopher Robin.

"That does appear to be true," agreed Pooh.

As Christopher Robin discussed the bees with Rabbit, Pooh watched them buzzing around. To him, they looked just as busy — and just as happy — as he and his friends had been when they helped Rabbit. Though he wasn't quite sure, he thought that perhaps the amount of bees in Rabbit's garden was somehow related to the amount of honey there could be.

"Perhaps you would consider these bees your tiniest team of garden helpers, Rabbit," suggested Pooh. "Because what they do makes them the biggest team of honey-makers. And honey-makers make some of us very happy indeed."

Rabbit opened his mouth to object, but was interrupted by a rumble from Pooh Bear's tummy.

Rabbit sighed and shook his head. "It takes many bees to make a hive, just like it takes many friends to make a garden grow." Then he smiled. "The bees can stay."

"That's the spirit, Rabbit!" said Christopher Robin. "Let's hear it for teamwork!"

"And honey," added Pooh.